Volcanoes
and other forces of nature
A LEGO® ADVENTURE IN THE REAL WORLD

Wow! Earth is full of awesome power! I lava good book.

📖 **SCHOLASTIC**

New York Toronto London Auckland
Sydney Mexico City New Delhi Hong Kong

Welcome LEGO fans!

LEGO® Minifigures show you the world in a unique nonfiction program.

This book is part of a program of LEGO® nonfiction books, with something for all the family, at every age and stage. LEGO nonfiction books have amazing facts, beautiful real-world photos, and minifigures everywhere, leading the fun and discovery.

To find out about the books in the program, visit www.scholastic.com

ISBN 978-1-338-14913-5

10 9 8 7 6 5 4 3 2 1   17 18 19 20 21

Printed in the U.S.A.   40   First edition, July 2017

Contents

Build it!
There are plenty of ideas for epic builds as you read through this book.

Play it!
Look out for these great ideas for minifigure action. Create adventures of your own!

You go right ahead. I think I might stay in this volcano crawler!

Let's go! I have a feeling this volcano is going to blow and I want to be part of the action!

Extreme Earth

Our planet can be a wild place. Volcanoes ooze sizzling hot lava, the ground shakes, and the weather can be pretty wild, too. All sorts of incredible people study our ever-changing planet to help keep us safe. Sometimes they have to get pretty close to the action!

I'm a volcanologist! My job is to study volcanoes. Stand back, this one is ready to erupt!

Seismologists study how and why the Earth moves. I'm taking this sample back to the lab to test it!

Earth just can't stay still. Movements of or under Earth's crust, its top layer, can cause volcanoes and earthquakes. Movements up in the atmosphere, the gases high in the air, cause crazy weather! Welcome to a world of extremes!

Something's boiling inside this mountain.

I'll look for clues to find out if a quake is about to shake.

Ahoy there! I'll let you know if a tsunami is coming.

Volcanic eruption
Boiling rock from inside the Earth shoots out of a volcanic mountain and spits fire and ash high into the sky.

Earthquake
When rock moves in the crust and deeper underground, the ground may shake and shudder. This is called an earthquake.

Tsunami
Massively long, powerful waves that can drench the land are called tsunamis. They may be triggered by earthquakes.

A wallop of wind, rain, and waves, hurricanes are very foul weather.

I can't twist like a tornado—they're tutu fast for me.

Blizzards last for hours and cover everything in snow. I'm not hanging around!

Hurricane
A hurricane is a HUGE storm that starts over the ocean. When it hits land, it can bend trees and cause flooding.

Tornado
A twisting column of air that touches the ground, tornadoes have wind speeds of up to 300 miles per hour (480 km/h).

Blizzard
Wild wintry weather with strong winds and huge dumps of whirling and swirling snow is called a blizzard.

7

Hot, liquid rock called magma boils and bubbles beneath the Earth's crust. When the pressure builds up, ka-BOOM! A volcano blows its top, and magma blasts through a crack in the crust.

FIRE FOUNTAIN

Lava jets called fire fountains shoot straight up. In 1986, one on Izu-Oshima Island, Japan, reached a height of 5,250 feet (1,600 m).

The word "volcano" comes from Vulcan, the ancient Roman god of fire.

1. Under pressure
Magma becomes less dense than the rock around it. It rises and pressure builds.

2. Pop goes the volcano
Sizzling magma spews out of a vent in the volcano. Once magma erupts, it is called lava.

3. A river of red
Red-hot lava flows down the sides, covering everything in its path.

VOLCANO FACTS

Biggest: Tamu Massif, under the Pacific Ocean
Loudest eruption: Krakatoa, 1883—it's still the loundest sound ever
Most famous: Mount Vesuvius in 79 CE, it completely buried the Roman town of Pompeii

BIG BELCH

Volcanoes shoot out lava, but they can also spew out showers of hot rocks or burning ash, or even clouds of stinky gases.

Get 'em while they're hot . . . NOT! When lava cools down, it hardens into rock.

Volcanic rocks are smooth and shiny, and they have crystals inside. Ooooh!

Lava

Hot stuff coming through! An oozing river of lava can reach temperatures of up to 2,200°F (1,200°C). It's not just hot, it's fast, too, flowing at up to 40 miles per hour (65 km/h).

I'm glad we're not working on the Stromboli volcano. It's been erupting for 2,000 years!

Phew! Doesn't it ever want a day off?

Boom!
Sometimes volcanoes shoot out lumps of molten rock called lava bombs.

Pahoehoe lava
Thin and runny, pahoehoe lava has a smooth or gently rippled surface when it cools to a solid.

Hmm, click, whirrr!

Build it!
Build a drone to get closer to the eruption.

Go with the flow
An erupting volcano may start by spewing out runny pahoehoe lava. Later on, the lava can thicken into aa lava.

Rivers of volcanic mud called lahars are almost as dangerous as lava. They can set hard like concrete.

Hmmm, what type of lava is that? It's too hot for me, but my drone can get really close and collect some data.

Aa lava
Pronounced "ah-ah," this type of lava is stickier than pahoehoe lava and has a jagged surface when solid.

Pillow lava
Imagine squeezing toothpaste from a tube. That's exactly how underwater volcanoes release their pilllow lava.

Volcano types

Volcanoes can be extinct (won't erupt again) or dormant (might erupt again). Active volcanoes are the ones to watch out for—they can erupt at any time!

Tengger massif
What's more awe-inspiring than one volcano? FIVE volcanoes together—like the Tengger massif in Indonesia, seen here.

CALDERA
If a volcano collapses in on itself after erupting, it creates a sunken crater called a caldera.

The biggest volcano in our solar system is Olympus Mons on Mars. I thought space would be nice and quiet . . .

Just out of curiosity, what's that rover doing? This is our volcano!

Beep beep!

Build it!
Make a volcano with a fountain of bricks as lava.

READY FOR ACTION
The ash clouds rising above some of the volcanoes show that they are active and could erupt.

There are 1,500 active volcanoes on land in the world. I like being active, but I prefer Zumba to magma!

CRATER
The crater is the mouth of the volcano where the eruption occurs.

Stratovolcano
A stratovolcano is a tall, steep cone with a small top, made from layers of lava and ash.

Shield volcano
This dome-shaped volcano has wide, gently sloping sides made from runny lava.

Cinder cone volcano
This volcano has steep sides, wide craters, and shoots out tiny rocks called lapilli.

Supervolcanoes

Imagine a volcano so loaded with magma that its eruption would be thousands of times bigger than any regular volcano. That's a supervolcano! But don't panic, the last supervolcano eruption was 74,000 years ago—phew!

Yellowstone hot springs

Yellowstone National Park is actually an active supervolcano. It last erupted 640,000 years ago. The heat from that eruption still powers the park's geysers and hot springs.

I'm so excited to hike through Yellowstone.

Are you sure the supervolcano isn't going to blow?

Hello! What are you doing?

I'm keeping a close eye on it. We don't think it's going to blow any time soon.

Rumble rumble

Hey! What's that rumble?

What a great view of Old Faithful! Better keep out of the way. I don't want to get into hot water!

Argghh! It must be the supervolcano. It's about to erupt!

Come back, it's just a hungry bear!

Old Faithful!
Geysers can blast magma-heated water more than 100 feet (30.5 m) into the air. Old Faithful, located in Yellowstone, shoots thousands of gallons of water into the air roughly every 90 minutes.

15

Underwater volcanoes

Most of the volcanic eruptions on Earth actually take place in the ocean depths. There may be more than 5,000 active underwater volcanoes belching out boiling hot lava right now!

Ocean explosion!
Underwater volcanoes sometimes shoot lava and ash high into the air above the water. As the rock falls back, it can pile up, making new islands above the water.

The water by volcanic chimneys is hot enough to melt lead and is hugely poisonous.

And I thought sharks were the scariest things down here!

ISLANDS

Many islands are formed by volcanic eruptions. The islands of Hawaii are all made from volcanoes.

Build it!

Your divers need an awesome submarine to explore undersea volcanoes. Add plenty of extras to help them.

Periscope

Clawhands

Lights

Propeller

Radar

Headlight

Smoky stacks

Magma heats seawater that leaks under the ocean floor. When the water rises and cools, minerals inside it make black smokers.

Home sweet home

Black smokers belch out bubbling clouds of hot, mineral-rich water. Strange creatures like to live there, from eyeless shrimps to hairy crabs!

Build it bigger!

Create an ocean floor dotted with volcanoes. There might be some black smokers nearby. Who (or what) lives there?

VOLCANOLOGISTS AT WORK

Volcanologists collect lava and rock samples and measure volcanic activity. The edge of the volcano is their science lab!

PLAY IT!
Take your volcanologists to work on the slope of an active volcano. There's a rumbling . . . and it's not their tummies!

A volcanologist suits up in protective gear to keep safe from the extreme heat. Special heat-proof gloves and boots allow the scientists to walk around and handle hot volcanic rocks. Their work is vital. If they can predict an eruption, they can make sure everyone is out of the way.

Volcanologists collect samples and data, and try to figure out just when the volcano will next erupt. When a volcano erupts, crystals form inside it. Layers of crystals can show exactly when it erupted in the past—it's a bit like measuring tree rings. Volcanologists can see if there is a pattern and predict the next blow. That sometimes means climbing inside the volcano! When working in the field, things can really start to heat up!

Did you know lava can reach temperatures of up to 2,200°F (1,200°C)? That's super sizzling.

A hard hat protects against any lava zooming out of the volcano.

There's lots to learn from extinct volcanoes, too.

I don't want my ice cream to melt. Back to the lab for me!

Play it! Here are some ideas . . .

1 What vehicle will your minifigures take?

2 Do they need a helicopter for a good view?

3 Is it about to blow? Run!

Ring of Fire

Our Earth doesn't have a solid surface. The crust is divided into plates that fit together like a jigsaw puzzle. The edge of the plates sometimes shift, and it's these restless areas that have volcanoes and earthquakes.

Step right up, and see seventy-five percent of the world's active volcanoes. It's a ring I can't master!

AUSTRALIA

NEW ZEALAND

LAND SHAKE

Much of the Pacific Plate is over the ocean, except for the eastern part that runs down North America.

NORTH AMERICA

Ring of Fire

Welcome to the most explosive area on Earth! 452 volcanoes form an arc around the Pacific Plate known as the Ring of Fire.

SOUTH AMERICA

Ninety percent of all earthquakes happen in the Ring of Fire.

HIGH AND MIGHTY

Some of the highest volcanoes line the South American coast. Nevados Ojos del Salado is more than 22,500 feet (6,800 m) high.

Delicious pie. I nearly cleaned my plate!

Funny, I've ju been learning about plate

So the Earth isn't a solid ball. Big, chunky plates on the top move across molten rock.

When a heavy plate meets a lighter plate, the heavy one slips right underneath.

BOOM! The molten rocks blast out of volcanoes at the surface.

You mean SPL a chocolate ca eruption. Sig

Earthquakes

When the Earth's plates move, they sometimes bump into each other or pull apart. The ground shudders as they move. Everything on the surface wobbles and shakes. It's an earthquake!

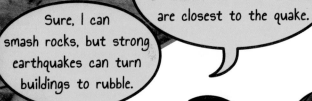

The shaking from most earthquakes lasts less than a minute. The worst shakes are closest to the quake.

Sure, I can smash rocks, but strong earthquakes can turn buildings to rubble.

After a quake, huge cracks can appear in the ground and roads can break. Let's patch it up!

The Earth's plates

There are seven main plates and several minor plates that make up the Earth. The plates are on average 50 miles (80 km) thick, and run over both land and ocean.

EARTHQUAKE FACTS

How many: About half a million every year, but only 100,000 that can be felt.

Most powerful: 9.5 magnitude, the 1960 Valdivia quake in Chile

Longest: Nearly 10 minutes—the 2004 Sumatra-Andaman quake

San Andreas fault

Earthquakes happen at faults, where the jagged edges of plates meet and move. The San Andreas fault runs down the west coast of the USA and is around 800 miles (1,300 km) long!

Normal faults

In a normal fault, two blocks of crust spread apart to make a gap or valley.

Thrust faults

One block of crust slides on top of another in a thrust, or reverse, fault. This sometimes forms mountains.

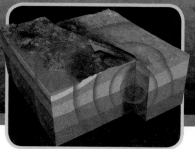

Strike-slip faults

Two blocks slide past each other without moving up or down. This can cause tiny tremors or huge quakes.

After a quake

Earthquakes can cause a lot of damage even after the first shock. Smaller earthquakes, called aftershocks, may come for months or even years.

Sure, the shaking is scary, but only about 100 earthquakes a year cause damage.

Rubble trouble

When an earthquake hits, buildings may fall. Scars appear where blocks of land move. Roads become uneven or crack. Even streams and rivers may change course.

Earthquake proof

Some of the world's most famous buildings are specially designed to survive quakes. The Landmark Tower is a tiny bit flexible so it will sway rather than topple over!

The Richter Scale: How to measure the strength of an earthquake

0-2	3	4	5	6	7	8
MICRO	**MINOR**	**LIGHT**	**MODERATE**	**STRONG**	**MAJOR**	**GREAT**
Not felt by people.	No building damage.	Objects may shake.	Objects fall to the floor.	Buildings are damaged.	Buildings may fall.	Damage to large area.

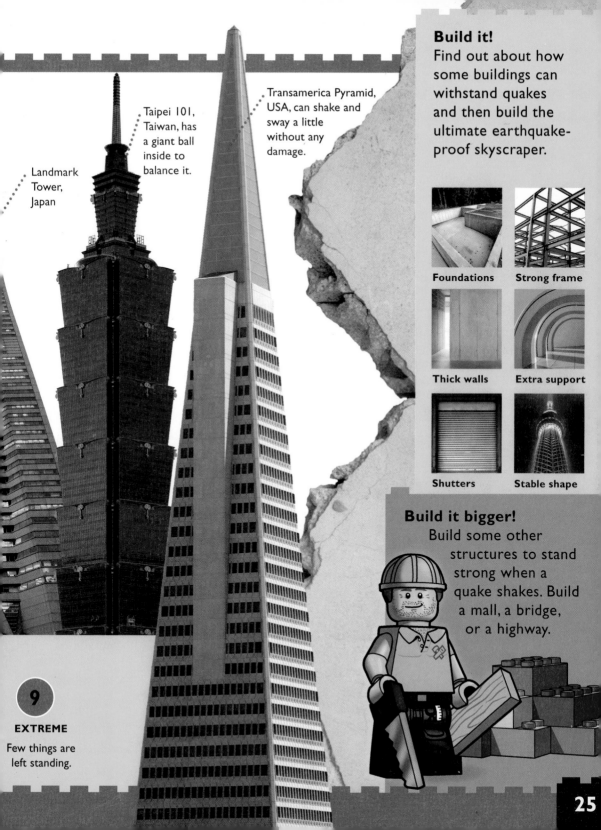

Landmark Tower, Japan

Taipei 101, Taiwan, has a giant ball inside to balance it.

Transamerica Pyramid, USA, can shake and sway a little without any damage.

Build it!
Find out about how some buildings can withstand quakes and then build the ultimate earthquake-proof skyscraper.

Foundations

Strong frame

Thick walls

Extra support

Shutters

Stable shape

Build it bigger!
Build some other structures to stand strong when a quake shakes. Build a mall, a bridge, or a highway.

9

EXTREME

Few things are left standing.

Seismologist
A scientist who

WHAT'S SHAKING?

Seismologists use special instruments to measure the strength of waves shaking the Earth. They also study tsunamis and landslides caused by earthquakes.

PLAY IT!
An earthquake strikes your brick city. You're in charge! What will you do?

Right now, seismologists are finding out what's happening under your feet! They're experts in what our planet is made from and how it moves, particularly the movements of Earth's plates. They study seismic waves—the waves of energy that spread out during an earthquake—and the tsunamis and landslides that follow.

Seismologists are the ultimate rock hounds! All around the world, they examine the ground, collect rock samples, and take them back to the lab. By studying all sorts of rocks, seismologists can help figure out where and when the next earthquakes may happen. They can let people know as soon and as much as they can. It's groundbreaking work!

Gas and oil companies use seismologists to help them find safe places to drill.

I'll bet those science folks know a whole lot about a whole lot of rocks!

Did someone say rock? I'm READY to ROCK!

Play it! Here are some ideas ...

1 Check out the damage to your city.

2 Start rebuilding, bigger and better than before.

3 Are your buildings quake-proof?

Landslides

Watch out! Winds caused by landslides can take the leaves right off the trees!

Earthquakes, volcanoes, and rainstorms can all loosen rocks and soil until they start to slip down a slope. Landslide! It can flow at 186 miles per hour (300 km/h).

Mount St. Helens
The volcano Mount St. Helens, in WA, erupted in 1980. One of the biggest ever landslides flowed for 14 miles (23 km).

Mudslide
After a huge rainstorm or snowmelt, muddy soil may rush down a hill carrying trees or even houses.

How many: about 300,000 each year

Most powerful: Ningxia, China, in 1920 destroyed entire villages

Strange but true: Mars and Venus have many landslides, too.

In the ocean, an earthquake may start an underwater landslide.

And the underwater landslide may start a tsunami.

Soil creep

Landslides may be as slow as 0.004 in. (0.1 mm) a year. They are caused by gravity and when the land freezes and thaws.

Sinkholes

Over thousands of years, water dissolves rock very, very slowly. Sometimes a cave forms. Suddenly, the ground opens up. Help! A sinkhole!

A robot explored one sinkhole in Mexico as practice for exploring one of Jupiter's moons!

Dude, where's my car?
This sinkhole in Minnesota swallowed a car! Florida, which sits on limestone, is famous for sinkholes. Limestone dissolves more than other rock over time.

Build it!
Create a robot equipped with cameras to explore a sinkhole.

Great Blue Hole

This mega underwater sinkhole off the coast of Belize is 984 feet (300 m) wide and 410 feet (125 m) deep. Many sea creatures live inside it.

Tsunamis

Super-sized ocean waves are called tsunamis. They can reach 100 feet (30 m) high and speed across the ocean at 500 miles per hour (800 km/h) —as fast as an airplane.

Wave of destruction

Tsunamis are most often caused by earthquakes or volcanoes. The ocean floor moves, causing the water to rise into a mega wave.

What happens next?

Tsunami waves can pound the coast for two hours. The waves gobble up islands, crush buildings, and drag boats ashore.

Tsunami alert

Scientists use detectors to check earthquake activity and warn people in tsunami-prone areas to get to safety.

TSUNAMI EVACUATION ROUTE

WALL OF WATER

As a tsunami nears the coast, it sucks in more water and gets even bigger. It then hits the shore with enormous power.

TSUNAMI FACTS

How many: Two big tsunamis per year, on average

Most powerful: 2004 Indian Ocean tsunami; it hit 14 countries

Strange but true: Tsunami debris can wash up on the other side of the world, up to five years later.

Did you know the tops of tsunami waves move faster than the bottoms do?

A tsunami can cross the Pacific Ocean in just one day. In that case, I'm sailing right out of here.

2509

Weird weather

The Sun makes all our planet's weather—even storms! The Sun heats the Earth by different amounts. Masses of warm and cold air move from place to place, causing winds that bring all sorts of weather. Check out these crazy weather events!

Glider pilots like to "surf" the huge cloud waves, using the wind to speed them along!

Hail-o there! The largest hailstone ever weighed nearly 2 pounds (0.88 kg). Ouch!

If it rains during a haboob then the rain turned to mud!

Cloud wave
Sometimes, clouds 600 miles (1,000 km) long sweep across northern Australia. They can move at 35 mph (55 km/h).

Giant hailstones
In 2010, a giant hailstone 8 inches (20 cm) wide fell in South Dakota. That's a bit like it was raining bowling balls!

Haboob!
In Sudan, sand from the Sahara desert is picked up in a storm and moves across cities like a 3,300-foot (1,000-m) dust wall

The windiest city in the world is Wellington, New Zealand.

Farmers have to bring animals indoors during ash storms. It's a bit of a squeeze!

The ice layer in the worst-ever storm was 8 inches (20 cm) thick. Get your skates on!

In 2010, hundreds of small fish fell from the sky in Australia!

Clouds of ash

In 2010, a volcano in Iceland erupted, sending a cloud of ash over Europe. Airplanes were grounded for six days.

Ice-out!

An extreme ice storm hit a huge area of North America in 2017, causing thunderstorms, tornadoes, and a lot of ice.

It's raining frogs!

In 2005, the people of Serbia went hopping mad when thousands of frogs fell out of the sky!

WHAT'S THE WEATHER LIKE?

Meteorologists gather data and put it together to make a weather forecast.

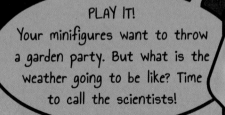

PLAY IT!
Your minifigures want to throw a garden party. But what is the weather going to be like? Time to call the scientists!

Scientists called meteorologists can predict the future! They know what the weather will be like, when it will change—and they even know why it happens. Meteorologists collect data on temperature, wind speed, cloud level, air pressure, and more to find patterns in the weather. Satellites high in the sky send pictures from all over the world, so they can also see how the weather is moving.

Meteorologists use computers to help them understand the data and predict the weather. But they can still get it wrong. Weather can spring surprises, from a snowstorm that seems to come out of nowhere to a hurricane that fizzles out before it really gets going. Better pack an umbrella, just in case,

Satellites up in space send down weather information to meteorologists on Earth.

I hope it doesn't rain today. I don't want to get rusty.

Meteorologists can predict the weather an hour, a day, or even weeks ahead.

My weather app tells me whether I need my snow tires. Thanks, science guys!

Play it! Here are some ideas . . .

1 Build a satellite and send it into space.

2 Analyze the data. Is that a storm coming?

3 It's sunny! Get the party started!

Hurricanes

This gigantic, swirling storm is nature at its fiercest. A hurricane's winds are speedy and strong, ripping off roofs, bending trees, and soaking the land with buckets of rain.

In a spin

A hurricane starts over warm ocean waters. Storm clouds build, picking up speed as the hurricane twists and turns toward land.

> How do hurricanes see? With one eye!

THE EYE

The stormy winds spin around a calmer center called the eye. It can be 30 miles (48 km) wide.

The Saffir-Simpson scale:
Rates the strength of a hurricane based on its speed

1	**2**	**3**	**4**	**5**
74–95 mph (119–153 km/h) Dangerous high winds	96–110 mph (154–177 km/h) Widespread damage	111–129 mph (178–208 km/h) Major storm, serious damage	130–156 mph (209–251 km/h) A catastrophe, severe damage	157 mph (252 km/h) and above Near total destruction

Hold on tight! Aircraft study and track hurricanes to let people know when they're coming.

HURRICANE FACTS

Strongest: Hurricane Patricia in 2015 off the coast of Mexico

Longest: Hurricane John, blowing in the Pacific Ocean in 1994 for 31 days

Strange but true: A huge hurricane on Jupiter, bigger than Earth itself, has been swirling for hundreds of years.

Storm surge

Traveling at least 74 miles per hour (119 km/h), a hurricane is bad enough. But when it strikes land, it can also bring surges of flood water 20 feet (6 m) high.

The word "hurricane" comes from a Native American word for an evil spirit of the wind.

Hurricane hunters

Oh, no! There's a plane flying straight toward a hurricane. Don't worry, the crew are hurricane hunters. They're on a mission to get up close to the storm and find out where it's heading.

Super plane

Hurricane hunters zoom through stormy skies in amazing, specially built, super-tough planes. They are packed with weather-testing equipment. Extra fuel tanks also help them travel long distances.

Into the hurricane

The hurricane hunters release sensors to gather data. The sensors head straight into the hurricane clouds and send data back to the crew.

Five brave crew members from the US Air Force fly each plane.

DROPSONDES

The sensors are called dropsondes. They have parachutes on the top to help them drift into the eye of the hurricane.

Build it!
Ready, storm chasers? Build a hurricane-hunting plane. Load it up with gadgets!

Extra fuel tank   **Radar**

Computers   **Strong frame**

Cockpit   **Cargo space**

HURRICANE PLANE
The hunters' planes can fly at 466 miles per hour (745 km/h).

Mapping the weather
Hurricane hunters send data back to weather forecasters on the ground. Their infomation helps people to stay safe.

Build it bigger!
Build a whole fleet of hurricane hunter planes and an airbase to house them.

Tornadoes

A tornado is a thundercloud in a very bad mood. These funnels of spinning air are also known as "twisters." They usually swirl by quickly, but their awesome wind speeds can leave a trail of destruction.

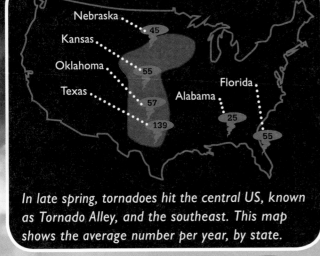

In late spring, tornadoes hit the central US, known as Tornado Alley, and the southeast. This map shows the average number per year, by state.

Nebraska 45
Kansas
Oklahoma 55
Texas 57
139
Alabama 25
Florida 55

How tornadoes form

Cold air and warm air meet during a thunderstorm. If winds change direction and speed up, they churn the air into a spinning tube-like cloud. If a funnel drops out of the cloud and touches the ground, it's a tornado.

TORNADO FACTS

Longest: Most tornadoes touch down for only a few minutes, but some extreme storms twist for up to an hour!

Strange but true: Tornadoes can carry away refrigerators, roofs, cars, and heavy machines.

DIRECTION
Most tornadoes spin counter-clockwise.

Widest ever
The widest tornado on record is the El Reno tornado in Oklahoma in 2013. It was 2.6 miles (4.2 km) wide at its peak and very, very strong.

COLOR
Tornadoes look gray because they have picked up dust and debris.

Whooshing winds inside a tornado move as fast as 318 mph (511 km/h). That's too fast for me!

RIDING THE STORM

Some pro stormchasers build super vehicles to keep them safe. These cars are solid and sturdy and won't blow over. Some can even be bolted down. Now, that's a wild ride!

The stormchasers in Tornado Alley have a problem—their vehicle has broken down. Can you build them a new one? You'd better build fast, there's a twister coming . . .

A big storm is on the way! Most people take cover, but stormchasers head right for the middle of it. There might actually be days of just hanging around and waiting when a storm is due, but as soon as it hits, the stormchasers leap into action.

Stormchasers hunt down extreme weather to help us all learn more about it. More information about weather patterns and storm conditions can help people to prepare better. Stormchasers follow the latest weather data online and use radar to monitor the storm. They even have devices to send right up into a tornado to collect information! Many of their vehicles are also equipped with the latest video cameras so they can capture amazing images.

Stormchasers keep a close watch on all the latest weather data.

Let the pros chase storms. I'm heading out in the opposite direction!

I think I'd rather chase a storm than catch a stinky skunk!

Play it! Here are some ideas . . .

1 How can you build a super-strong vehicle?

2 What equipment does it need? Pack that camera!

3 Will you finish it in time?

Lightning storms

A US park ranger was hit by lightning SEVEN times . . . and survived! THAT'S a lot of strikes!

Every day, 8 million lightning strikes flash around the Earth. That's 100 times every second! Inside clouds, water droplets collide and create an electric charge, then ZAP! A flash of lightning.

Rumble of thunder

The heat from a flash of lightning sends shockwaves through the air. This creates a loud rumble. That's thunder! Sound travels slower than light. That's why we hear thunder after we see the flash of lightning.

Cloud to cloud

Most lightning never hits the Earth. Instead, it zips from cloud to cloud. This lightning can make the sky glow.

Cloud to ground

Sometimes lightning is attracted to something on the ground. It shoots down then bolts back up again.

Flashing upwards

Sometimes, lightning causes streaks in the sky, called red sprites, high above thunderclouds.

FLASH FACTS

Power: Each bolt of lightning can hold up to a billion volts of electricity.

How hot: A flash is five times hotter than the surface of the Sun!

How long: Lightning strikes usually last around 1 or 2 microseconds.

HIGH RISE

Lightning strikes the highest thing around. Many tall buildings have metal lightning rods on top. These safely carry the electric current to the ground.

That lightning storm is super-scary!

Don't be so chicken! The safest place to be in a lightning storm is inside. Yawn! I'm off to bed.

Volcanic lightning

Sometimes a volcano may produce lightning! It forms inside the ash clouds that erupt from the volcano.

Flooding

Floods cause more damage than any other force of nature. Heavy rain, huge waves, and melting snow may cause rushing water. Water can destroy buildings, take down trees, and ruin farmland.

In 2011, a coastal town in Australia was flooded and sharks swam down the streets!

Wow, I'm going to have to be extra street smart!

> Floods aren't all bad. The River Nile, in Egypt, used to flood every year, making the soil rich for growing crops.

Build it!
Your brick city is at risk from rising flood waters. Build some ways to protect the town and keep the people safe!

Sandbags

Trees

Sea walls

Water gates

Weirs

Canals

Monsoon season
A monsoon is a wind that changes direction because of the season. In Asia, the summer monsoon brings heavy rain that can cause massive floods.

Build it bigger!
In some flood-prone areas, big walls called dams help control flooding. Build the tallest, strongest, best dam ever.

Hurricane floods
Windy hurricanes can also bring heavy rains. They can flood whole towns and cities, turning roads into rivers.

Tsunami floods
Tsunamis are huge sea waves that crash onto land. They can travel as far as 10 miles (16 km) inland, causing floods.

Wildfires

After a hot, dry spell of weather, all it takes is a tiny spark to set the ground alight. Before you know it, whoosh! A wildfire can move at 14 miles per hour (23 km/h), burning up everything in its path.

Fire starters
Lightning or volcanic eruptions can cause wildfires. However, most wildfires are started by people. Many countries don't allow campfires during dry seasons.

There are more than 50,000 wildfires in the US every year.

A wildfire needs fuel, oxygen, and a heat source to burn.

There's fuel everywhere. Just look at all the trees and brush.

Yep, only Sparky here has more bark.

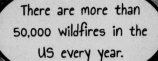

Flaming forest

In 2016, 2,300 square miles (6,000 square km) of forest burned down in Canada. 2,400 buildings were destroyed.

Water drop

Special planes called air tankers scoop up water from the sea or lakes and dump it on fires to help put them out.

AFTER THE FIRE

Forest fires sometimes get rid of plant diseases and pests, leaving the ground healthy for plants to grow again.

So, add something hot, like a lightning strike, and then WHOOSH! We've got work to do!

The wind brings the oxygen the fire needs to grow.

A brave hero who

LET'S FIGHT THAT FIRE!

Being a firefighter is all about teamwork. The crew works together with some cool tools to tackle the flames and keep people safe.

PLAY IT!
Emergency! There's a forest fire, and it's spreading . . . fast! Send your firefighters out to the rescue!

It's an emergency! Sirens wailing and lights flashing, the fire engine speeds to the rescue. When forces of nature like hurricanes and earthquakes strike, firefighters are right at the heart of the action. Their big job is still fighting flames, but they are trained to do many other important tasks, too.

Most firefighters have medical skills so they can help people who are injured or hurt. Firefighters also lead search-and-rescue teams to find people who might be trapped. They can deal with hazards like fallen power lines and messy chemical spills that might cause even more trouble. Alongside the police and emergency rescue teams, firefighters keep people safe in dangerous and scary situations.

Help, help! Fire!

A firefighter's protective clothing can keep him or her safe in temperatures of up to 1,000°F (537°C).

A fire hose can shoot out 95 gallons (359 liters) of water per minute.

We'll have that fire out soon!

Play it! Here are some ideas . . .

1	Are your firefighters in a truck or a plane?	2	Do they tell minifigures to move to safety?	3	Will they put the fire out before it hits the town?

Snowstorms

Brrr, it's cold outside! An extreme snowstorm is called a blizzard. It lasts for several hours and high winds blow snow everywhere.

A snowstorm becomes a blizzard when the wind blows at more than 35 miles per hour (56 km/h).

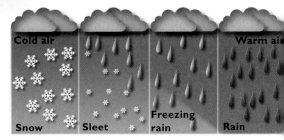

Cold air | Warm air

Snow | Sleet | Freezing rain | Rain

Making a snowstorm

When it's really cold outside, water in the air freezes into ice crystals, instead of rain. The crystals crash into each other, stick together, and get heavier. It's snow time!

I love blizzards, but they do mess up my hair . . .

Build it!
Can you design a slick snowmobile to beat a blizzard? Here are some ideas to make your snowmobile go!

Flashing lights

Heavy tracks

Skis

Windshield

Headlights

Walkie talkie

ICICLES

If the temperature goes up and down, drips of ice can melt and then freeze again. Layer by layer, spiky icicles form.

Get ready!
Deep snow makes getting around difficult, and a blizzard can knock out power supplies for days. So, it's important to be prepared.

Water

Food

Shovel

Power

Phone

Batteries

Chains

Flashlight

Jump leads

Ice scraper

Build it bigger!
Some minifigures are stuck in the snow! Build a snowplow and other special vehicles to clear the way.

Avalanche!

The snow on the mountain starts to move. It picks up more snow as it tumbles down. It speeds downhill faster and faster, growing all the time. Soon it is powerful enough to tear down trees as it falls. It's an avalanche!

Super slide

Avalanches often happen when a heavy snowfall falls on icy ground. The snow then slips down the ice. On a steep mountain, it can fall quickly.

Yodel-lay-he!

Shhh, you'll start an avalanche!

Don't be silly. No one can sing loud enough to shake the snow off a mountain!

Phew! In that case, Yodel-lay-he-hoo!

AVALANCHE FACTS

Biggest: A huge avalanche at Mt. Huascaran in Peru ran for 11 miles (17 km).

Strange but true: Snowflakes are light and fluffy, but an avalanche is more like a white river of wet cement. When it stops, it sets firm.

Shifting snow

Skiers can cause avalanches if they ski over loose snow. Skiers should always let someone know where they are going.

Blast it!

Starting an avalanche on purpose seems like a bad idea! However, blasting loose snow out of the way can stop a bigger, more dangerous avalanche.

Avalanches can reach speeds of up to 80 miles per hour (130 km/h). Yikes!

When the forces of nature cause chaos, you need amazing vehicles that can handle anything. These mighty machines are tough enough to handle some pretty unstable ground!

Caterpillar tracks help this volcano crawler travel over rocky ground without tipping over.

Skis help me slide over snowy ground. I'm on my way!

Snow problem

Some snowmobiles have tracks on the back, as well as skis, to help them travel over icy ground.

A tow hook at the front can pull out another vehicle that's stuck in the mud or in water. Heave!

Now everyone is safe, I'll have this mess cleared up in no time.

Build it!
What features does a rescue vehicle need? Here are some ideas to help you build the most awesome rescue vehicle.

Big wheels

Tracks

Skis

Digger bucket

Flashing light

Tow rope

Build it bigger!
Make a command station for your rescue team. You'll need space for all your vehicles plus a control center.

Big foot
Thanks to its huge wheels, an all-terrain vehicle can drive over bumpy ground, even if there isn't a road.

Clearing up
Sometimes nature creates a big mess. Diggers can scoop up rock and rubble and lift it away.

Helicopter rescue

They're small, fast, and can fly virtually anywhere—helicopters are the ultimate rescue vehicle. They can hover while they search and then lower rescuers and equipment to the ground or sea, even in bad weather!

STRAIGHT UP

This spinning rotor allow the helicopter to take of and land vertically, which means it can land in a small area with no runwa

SUPER MOVER

Helicopters can move forward, backward, side-to-side, as well as hover.

NASA wants to send an unmanned helicopter to Mars to search out the volcanic action there!

LOWER ME DOWN!

If the helicopter can't land, then the crew are lowered down to the rescue on ropes with their equipment!

Phew, it's smelly when that volcano belches! Let's not hover around here for too long!

FIREFIGHTERS

Helicopters may carry huge buckets of water or special chemicals that they can drop to help put out fires.

RESCUE SAUVETAGE

We have enough volcanic action here on Earth to keep us occupied!

The experts in this book have climbed to the top of my hero list!

Aftershock
A mini-quake that can happen right after a big earthquake.

Air tanker
An airplane that holds a tank of water that it drops onto forest fires to help put them out.

Ash
Black, powdery material that is left over after something burns up.

Time for me ... Now I know what a ...ologist does, I've got ...re data to collect!

Black smoker
An underwater chimney that belches out super-hot water and chemicals.

Blizzard
A huge snowstorm with very strong winds that lasts for hours.

Caldera
The hole that a volcano makes when it falls in on itself after exploding.

Crater
The bowl-shaped structure around the opening of a volcano where magma and lava erupt from.

Crust
The outer part of our Earth that we can see and stand on.

Dam
A barrier, or wall, that stops the flow of water.

Dropsonde
A weather instrument that is dropped from an airplane with a parachute attached to test the air.

Fault
A crack in the Earth where plates meet one another.

Geyser
A hot spring where boiling water explodes regularly into the air.

Haboob
A violent wind that picks up sand from the desert and blows it across the land.

Hail
Balls of ice that may rain down from clouds, often during a thunderstorm.

Landslide
When rocks, mud, and debris slide down a hill or mountain.

Lava
Fiery or molten rock that has exploded out of a volcano.

Magma
The boiling hot, liquid rock that lies under the Earth's crust.

Meteorologist
A scientist who studies the weather.

Minerals
Solid, natural substances that are not made from animals or plants. Minerals are found in rocks and soil.

Monsoon
A seasonal wind in Asia or Africa that can bring heavy rain.

NASA
The US Space Organization— National Aeronautics and Space Administration.

Plate
The large pieces of the Earth's crust that fit together like a jigsaw puzzle.

Richter scale
A scale used to measure earthquake strength.

Saffir-Simpson scale
A way that scientists measure the strength of a hurricane by its wind speed.

Some books really drone on, but I think this one is more awesome than a supervolcano!

Satellite
A human-made machine that travels around the Earth in space, sending back information.

Seismologist
A scientist who studies everything to do with earthquakes.

Supervolcano
A gigantic volcano that is thousands of times more powerful than a regular volcano.

Volcanologist
A scientist who studies everything to do with volcanoes.

Index and credits

Index

Credits

For the LEGO Group: Peter Moorby Licensing Coordinator; Heidi K. Jensen Licensing Manager; Paul Hansford Creative Publishing Manager; Martin Leighton Lindhardt Publishing Graphic Designer
Photos © : cover center: AZ68/iStockphoto; cover bottom: Vershinin-M/iStockphoto; cover top right sign texture: ISMODE/iStockphoto; back cover top left: Solarseven/Dreamstime; back cover center top: 4nadia/iStockphoto; 1: Claudio Rossol/Shutterstock; 2-3 background: Ammit Jack/Shutterstock; 2-3 broken walls: muratart/Shutterstock; 4-5 background: photography by Sanchai Loongroong/Getty Images; 6-7 backgroun: loops7/iStockphoto; 6 bottom left: SalvoV/iStockphoto; 6 bottom center: Claudiad/iStockphoto; 6 bottom right: shannonstent/iStockphoto; 7 top right: voraorn/iStockphoto; 7 bottom left: NOAA; 7 bottom center: vicnt/iStockphoto; 7 bottom right: Dorin_S/iStockphoto; 8-9 background: Fotos593/Shutterstock; 8 bottom left: Eucagallery/iStockphoto; 8 bottom center: James Steidl/Dreamstime; 8 bottom right: Juliengrondin/Dreamstime; 10 top left: DPKuras/iStockphoto; 10 center right: mikeuk/iStockphoto; 10 bottom right: Justinreznick/iStockphoto; 11 top: Vershinin-M/iStockphoto; 11 bottom left: etvulc/iStockphoto; 11 bottom right: OAR/National Undersea Research Program/Science Source; 12-13 background: AvigatorPhotographer/iStockphoto; 13 bottom left: Cyrus Read/AVO/USGS; 13 bottom center: Wildnerdpix/iStockphoto; 13 bottom right: Amenohi/iStockphoto; 14-15 background: Kalyan V. Srinivas/Dreamstime; 16 bottom left: PeakMystique/iStockphoto; 16 left: Don King/Getty Images; 16-17 background: Dana Stephenson/Getty Images; 17 bottom left: B. Murton/Southampton Oceanography Centre/Science Source; 17 bottom right: Science Source; 17 right top left: Andreus/Dreamstime;

17 right top right reef: Andrey_Kuzmin/Shutterstock; 17 right top right claw: Kirsty Pargeter/Dreamstime; 17 center right: Waynerd/iStockphoto; 17 right center left: pixone/iStockphoto; 17 right bottom left: Evannovostro/Shutterstock; 17 right bottom right: tavizta/Shutterstock; 18 top icons and throughout: clusterx/Fotolia; 18 top left: Vershinin-M/iStockphoto; 18 top right: Hawaiian Volcano Observatory/USGS; 18 bottom left: Deborah Bergfeld/AVO/USGS; 18 bottom right: Tim Orr/USGS; 18-19 background: alexey_ds/iStockphoto; 20-21 background: NOAA/Science Source; 20-21 volcano icons: Andy_R/iStockphoto; 22-23 background: Kevin Schafer/Alamy Images; 22 top: Mopic/Shutterstock; 24-25 broken walls: muratart/Shutterstock; 24 center: fpolat69/Shutterstock; 24 right: Pabkov/Shutterstock; 25 left: GoranQ/iStockphoto; 25 center: Zack Frank/Shutterstock; 25 right top right: zhengzaishuru/Shutterstock; 25 right center left: lorenzo104/iStockphoto; 25 right center right: BeholdingEye/iStockphoto; 25 right bottom right: ZHUYIMING/iStockphoto; 25 right bottom left: Franck-Boston/iStockphoto; 26-27 background: SteveCollender/iStockphoto; 26 top right: Inga Spence/Science Source; 26 top left: argus/Shutterstock; 26 center left: Science Source; 26 center right: Naypong/Shutterstock; 28-29 background: Felipe Dana/AP Images; 28 bottom left background: Mac99/iStockphoto; 28 bottom right: BanksPhotos/iStockphoto; 28 bottom left sign:

YuSev/Shutterstock; 28 bottom center: WestWindGraphics/iStockphoto; 29 bottom left: Marccophoto/iStockphoto; 30-31 background: Brian Peterson/The Star Tribune/AP Images; 31 top left: DNY59/iStockphoto; 32-33 background: shannonstent/iStockphoto; 32 bottom left: ArtwayPics/iStockphoto; 32 bottom center: NOAA; 32 bottom right: Sieto/iStockphoto; 34-35 background: Minerva Studio/iStockphoto; 34 top left: AlesVeluscek/iStockphoto; 34 bottom center: zokru/iStockphoto; 34 bottom right: Pavliha/iStockphoto; 34 bottom left: Mick Petroff/NASA; 35 bottom center: Boyan Dimitrov/Shutterstock; 35 bottom right frog: Antagain/iStockphoto; 35 bottom right water: Mr_Twister/iStockphoto; 35 bottom left: narloch-liberra/iStockphoto; 36-37 background: danm12/Shutterstock; 36 top left: NOAA; 36 bottom left: Dreamstimepoint/Dreamstime; 36 top right: NOAA; 36 bottom right: Robert Adrian Hillman/Shutterstock; 38-39 background: NOAA; 40-41 background: behindlens/Shutterstock; 40-41 background: NOAA; 40 bottom left: XM Collection/Alamy Images; 41 left: NOAA; 41 right center right: NOAA; 41 right center left: NOAA; 41 right top right: NOAA; 41 right top left: tBoyan/iStockphoto; 41 right top right: Petrovich9/iStockphoto; 41 right bottom left: NOAA; 42-43 background: Minerva Studio/Shutterstock; 44-45 background: Minerva Studio/iStockphoto; 44 center background: mdesigner125/Shutterstock; 44 center: Ryan McGinnis/Alamy Images; 46-47 background: Strazkul/Dreamstime; 46 lightning: EvergreenPlanet/iStockphoto; 46 bottom left: sandsun/iStockphoto; 46 bottom center: LukaTDB/iStockphoto; 46 bottom right: Mikkel Juul Jensen/Bonnier Publications/Science Source; 47 bottom left: Olivier Vandeginste/Science Source; 48-49 background: Thor Jorgen Udvang/Shutterstock; 48 center: Laboo Studio/Shutterstock; 49 bottom left: Vincent

Laforet/The New York Times/AP Images; 49 right top left: KarenMassier/iStockphoto; 49 right top right: martinhosmar/iStockphoto; 49 right center left: JulieanneBirch/iStockphoto; 49 right center right: PPrat/iStockphoto; 49 right bottom left: tirc83/iStockphoto; 49 right bottom right: deimagine/iStockphoto; 49 bottom center:; 50-51 background: Mack2happy/Dreamstime; 50 top right: PhilLober/iStockphoto; 51 top: Arnaudhennebicq/Dreamstime; 51 bottom right: tuchkovo/iStockphoto; 52-53 background: Wustrow-K/iStockphoto; 52 top left: Pgiam/iStockphoto; 52 bottom left: Al Ungar/iStockphoto; 52 bottom left: Toa55/iStockphoto; 52 bottom right: SullivanPhotography/iStockphoto; 54-55 background: belterz/iStockphoto; 54 bottom right: herpens/iStockphoto; 55 top: Mr_Twister/iStockphoto; 55 shovel: wwing/iStockphoto; 55 generator: DonNichols/iStockphoto; 55 jumper cables: 4kodiak/iStockphoto; 55 ice scraper: Ilya_Starikov/iStockphoto; 55 snow tire: mladn61/iStockphoto; 55 flashlight: Diabluses/iStockphoto; 55 canned food: le_cyclope/iStockphoto; 55 batteries: AnthonyRosenberg/iStockphoto; 55 bottled water: thumb/iStockphoto; 55 phone: ET-ARTWORKS/iStockphoto; 55 right top left: 2ndLookGraphics/iStockphoto; 55 right top right: WesAbrams/iStockphoto; 55 right center left: Rhombur/iStockphoto; 55 right center right: shaunl/iStockphoto; 55 right bottom left: sara_winter/iStockphoto; 55 right bottom right: amphotora/iStockphoto; 56-57 background: StockShot/Alamy Images; 56-57 fence: Mikkel Bigandt/Shutterstock; 56-57 bottom snow: herpens/iStockphoto; 57 bottom left: koya79/iStockphoto; 57 center right: dolomite-summits/Shutterstock; 58-59 background: solarseven/

Shutterstock; 58 bottom right: diephosi/iStockphoto; 59 bottom left: Fodor90/iStockphoto; 59 bottom center: CHUYN/iStockphoto; 59 top left: Falcor/iStockphoto; 59 right top right: lovely shot/iStockphoto; 59 right center left: shaunl/iStockphoto; 59 right center right: stevecoleimages/iStockphoto; 59 right bottom left: MarkusBeck/iStockphoto; 59 right bottom right: loongar/iStockphoto; 60-61 background: valio84sl/iStockphoto; 60-61 helicopter: OliverChilds/iStockphoto.

All LEGO® illustrations by Paul Lee.

I can't believe this book is over! I'm going to read it again.